~4.00

MW00912809

AIDS

Andrew T. McPhee

Franklin Watts
A Division of Grolier Publishing
New York • London • Hong Kong • Sydney
Danbury, Connecticut

To everyone whose hands and hearts have created a panel for the AIDS quilt.
Their love, hope, and passion for a cure fuels us all.

Note to readers: Definitions for words in **bold** can be found in the Glossary at the back of this book. Some names and other details in this book have been changed to maintain the confidentiality of victims of HIV. The stories, however, are true, and the people involved in them are real.

Photographs ©: Impact Visuals: 19 (C. Jana Birchum), 25, 29 (Dan Habib), 20 (Dana Schuerholz); Medichrome/StockShop: 12; Peter Arnold Inc. 3, 10 (Manfred Kage), 21 (Leonard Lessin), 34 (Matt Meadows), 27 (SIU); Photo Researchers: 22 (Bill Bachman), 18 (Oscar Burriel/Latin Stock/SPL), cover (CNRI/SPL), 6 (Simon Fraser/SPL), 14 (David M. Grossman), 47 (Will & Deni McIntyre), 43 top (N. Durrell McKenna), 4 (Vanessa Vick); PhotoEdit: 3, 33 (Bill Aron), 13 (Myrleen Ferguson); Stock Boston: 43 bottom (Bob Daemmrich), 24 (Judy Gelles); The Image Works: 36 (B. Bachmann), 40 (Bob Daemmrich), 30 (Esbin-Anderson), 44 (Okoniewski), 41 (J. Sulley); Tony Stone Images: 8 (Hans Gelderblom), 16, 17 (Chris Noble), 39 (Manoj Shah).

The photograph on the cover shows HIV-infected immune cells as seen through an electron microscope.

Visit Franklin Watts on the Internet at: http://publishing.grolier.com

Library of Congress Cataloging-in-Publication Data

McPhee, Andrew T.
    AIDS / by Andrew T. McPhee
        p. cm.— (Watts Library)
    Includes bibliographical references and index.
    Summary: Discusses the disease AIDS, including its cause, potential sources of HIV infection, testing, and treatment.
    ISBN 0-531-11779-0 (lib. bdg.)   0-531-16528-0 (pbk.)
1. AIDS (Disease)—Juvenile literature. [1. AIDS (Disease) 2. Diseases] I. Title. II. Series.
RC155.5.S568 2000
616.97'92—dc21

99-045288
CIP

Contents

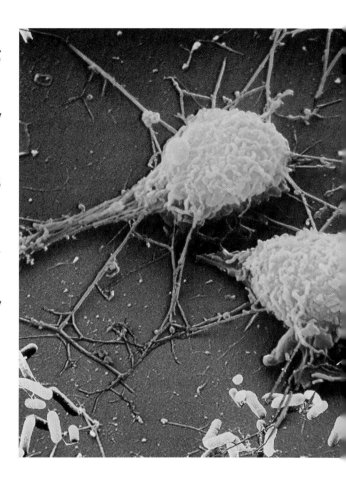

Panels of the AIDS Memorial Quilt lie stretched out in front of the Washington Monument in Washington, D.C. The Quilt normally travels around the United States in sections, but in 1996, the entire quilt was displayed. Every year, 1,000 new panels are added to the Quilt.

Chapter One

Focus on HIV

When spread out, the AIDS Memorial Quilt covers an area the size of sixteen football fields. The Quilt consists of more than 40,000 cloth panels—each one made in memory of someone who died of AIDS. Walking among the thousands of panels is an emotional experience. People walk silently among them, many wiping tears from their eyes. Parents hug, and then cry, when they find the panel they made for their child. Here and there, groups of people kneel in front of panels to remember lost friends or relatives. Over and over, visitors can be heard to say, "So many names. So many names."

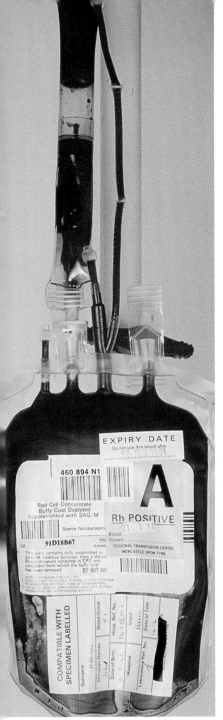

The blood in this bag is being transfused, or injected, into a patient.

More than 400,000 people in the United States have died of AIDS since the disease was identified in 1981. That's more people than the entire population of St. Louis, Missouri. What happened? How could a disease that nobody had heard of before 1981 kill so many people?

The Start of AIDS

When the first few patients developed signs of AIDS, doctors didn't know what the disease was. They didn't have a name for it or know how to treat it. In the beginning, doctors began to see patients suffering from illnesses that didn't usually make people sick—but for some reason, these patients were seriously ill. Some were dying of illnesses that were normally harmless. Scientists and doctors wanted to find out why.

They suspected that something was weakening the **immune** system of the sick people. The immune system is the body's army against illness and is made up of special cells and chemicals that fight disease. When the immune system is damaged, the body can get sick more easily. Even an ordinary cold can be dangerous when the body's defenses are down.

The doctors also noticed that some of the sick people knew each other. Some were friends who had shared needles for drugs. Some were lovers who had sexual contact with each other. Some had received blood **transfusions**,

6

in which blood from another person was injected into their veins. The doctors thought that whatever was weakening the immune system of their patients might be something that could be passed from one person to another. They began to look for an organism that could cause the mysterious infections they were seeing.

Most infections in humans are caused by bacteria or viruses. In 1984, after much research in the United States and throughout the world, two teams of scientists finally identified the new disease-causing virus. The virus eventually became known as **human immunodeficiency virus (HIV)**, the virus that causes AIDS.

HIV Close-Up

If you looked at HIV through a high-powered microscope, you might be able to see what looks like a clump of fuzzy tennis balls stuck to something that looks like a football. A closer look would reveal that the outside layer of the "tennis balls" is covered with curly threads. You might think that if you picked up one of the balls and threw it at a target, it would stick when it hit.

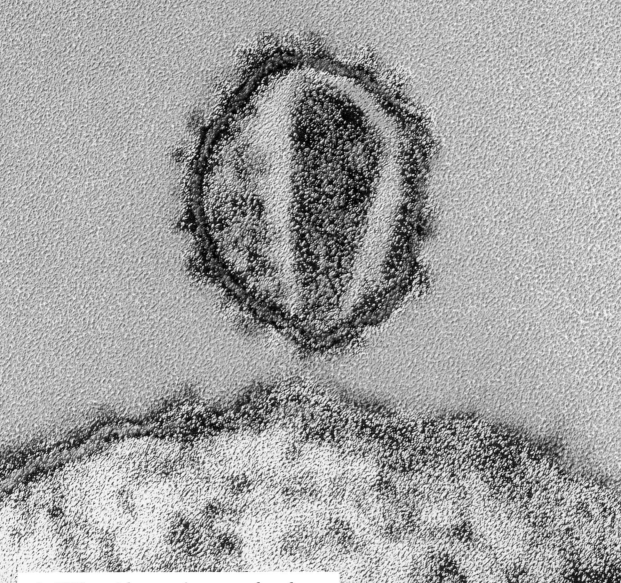

An HIV particle preparing to attach to the surface of a cell's membrane, seen through an extremely powerful instrument called a transmission electron microscope.

The "tennis balls" are particles of HIV sticking to a large cell. In a way, HIV *does* stick to the cells it attacks. The "curly threads" are specially shaped **proteins**—chemicals found in all plants and animals. Different viruses have different proteins on their surfaces. If a virus has the right kinds of proteins, it can attach to a cell. The proteins on the surface of HIV help it attach to infection-fighting cells such as **T cells**, an important part of the immune system.

After a virus sticks to a cell, it tries to get inside the cell. If the virus has the right proteins on its surface, it can pass through the cell's protective wall, called the cell membrane. Sometimes the virus then takes over the cell's command center, called the **nucleus**. The virus orders the cell to stop whatever it normally would be doing and to start manufacturing copies of the virus instead. The cell makes more and more copies of the virus—up to 2 million— until it dies and bursts open, sending the newly made virus particles into the body. Those virus particles then hook onto other cells and infect them.

HIV attacks two of the most important infection-fighting cells, also known as white blood cells—**macrophages** (MAK-roh-fay-jez) and T cells. These immune system cells protect the body against bacteria, viruses, and certain types of cancer. T cells are the lookouts of the immune system. They identify invaders, and call in reinforcements—macrophages and other immune defenders.

Macrophages wrap themselves around the invaders and then destroy them. As HIV spreads through the body, it knocks out

Infection Fighters

Macrophages wrap themselves around invaders such as bacteria. After the invaders are completely enclosed, a macrophage destroys them with special chemicals.

9

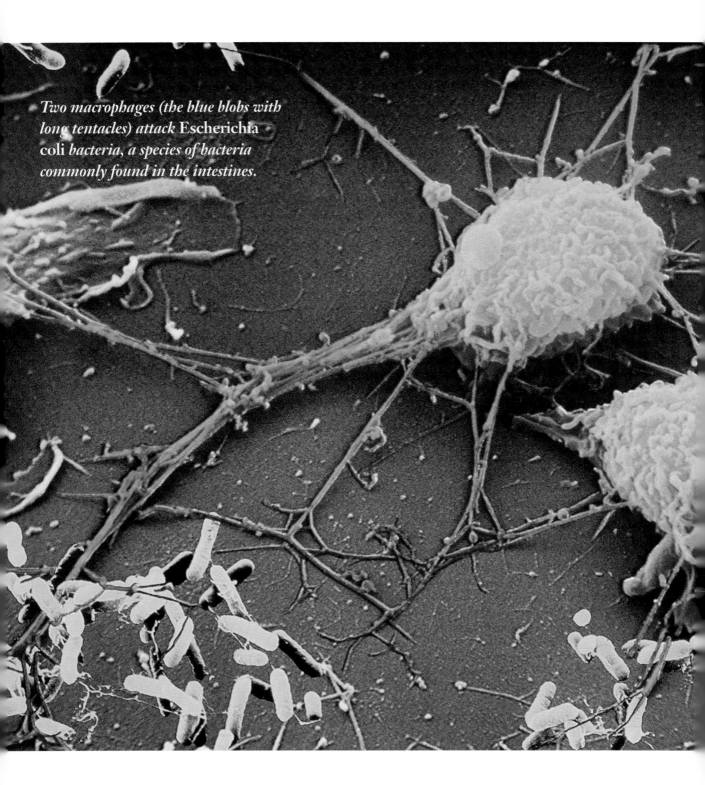

Two macrophages (the blue blobs with long tentacles) attack Escherichia coli *bacteria, a species of bacteria commonly found in the intestines.*

these defenses, which should be protecting the body against infection, and uses them to manufacture more viruses. That opens the door for other illnesses to move in.

How HIV Damages the Body

A few days after HIV enters the body, the number of HIV particles in the bloodstream skyrockets. At the same time, the number of T cells in the body drops to a dangerously low level.

An infected person may develop a fever, a rash, muscle aches, or a headache, but will usually begin to feel better within 3 weeks. That's because the immune system has begun to prepare for battle against the virus, and has made more T cells. Those T cells call in other types of immune system cells to attack and kill HIV. This defensive attack usually succeeds, but only for a while.

In most people, the immune system can control HIV for 8 to 10 years. This period—from the time of infection to the time a person begins to show signs of illness—is often called the **incubation period.**

Eventually, though, the immune system begins to wear out. HIV takes over more and more T cells. The number of HIV particles climbs, while the number of T cells drops.

A person is said to have AIDS when there are fewer than 200 T cells per cubic millimeter of blood. Healthy people usually have more than 1,000 T cells in that tiny amount of blood. AIDS is the final stage of an infection with HIV.

Battle Begins

The number of HIV particles in the blood typically increases quickly during the first 6 weeks following infection. Then, about 6 weeks after HIV enters the body, the number of T cells bounces back. The T cells can keep the virus from causing signs of disease for 8 to 10 years.

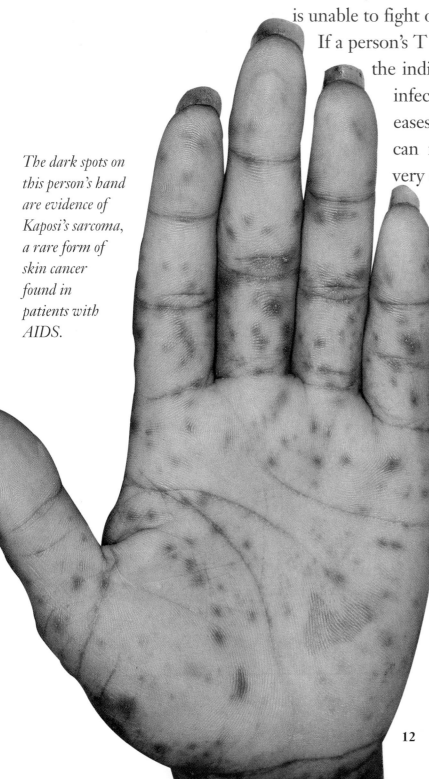

The dark spots on this person's hand are evidence of Kaposi's sarcoma, a rare form of skin cancer found in patients with AIDS.

During this final stage, the immune system is unable to fight outside infections effectively. If a person's T cell count drops below 100, the individual can suffer dangerous infections or cancers. Even diseases that are normally harmless can make a person with AIDS very sick.

For example, a lung infection called ***Pneumocystis carinii* pneumonia** may develop. So can **Kaposi's sarcoma**, a skin cancer rarely found in people with a healthy immune system but often seen among people with AIDS. **Tuberculosis**, a highly **contagious** lung disease, is also common among HIV-infected patients. After a person infected with HIV develops one of these conditions, death usually occurs within 2 years.

12

How HIV Does and Doesn't Spread

A person can pick up, or **contract**, HIV by coming into **direct contact** with the blood or body fluids of a person infected with HIV. In direct contact, the virus passes straight into the blood. This can happen when a person injects drugs with a needle containing the AIDS virus.

The virus can also pass through a person's **mucous membranes**—tissues that line the inside of the mouth, rectum, **genital tract**, urinary system, and other parts of the body. HIV commonly passes through mucous membranes during sex.

HIV can also pass from a mother to her child before or during childbirth. Recently infected mothers might have HIV in their breast milk. A baby can pick up HIV through breast-feeding from a woman infected with the virus.

A mother holds her infant, wrapped snugly in a towel. HIV can pass from an infected mother to her child during birth or breast-feeding.

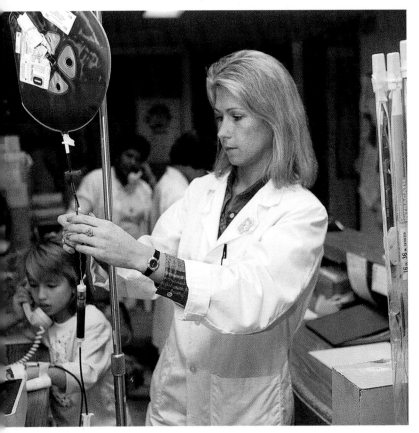

For several years after HIV was identified, many people contracted the virus from transfusions of blood containing HIV. People with a blood disease called **hemophilia** were at especially high risk of being infected. In 1985, blood banks in the United States began testing all donated blood for HIV, so today, getting a blood transfusion is extremely safe. There is almost no chance of contracting HIV through a blood transfusion in the United States and other developed countries.

A young patient receives a blood transfusion. Blood transfusions are now considered virtually free of HIV.

Hemophilia

Hemophilia is a condition in which a person's blood does not clot properly. Hemophiliacs—people with hemophilia—lack chemicals that help blood to clot and form scabs. As a result, these individuals do not stop bleeding as quickly as people with normal blood. Without care, they can bleed to death.

Hemophiliacs need regular transfusions of the chemicals that help blood clot. In the past, the only source of these chemicals was supplies of donated blood. Because some donated blood was infected with HIV during the 1980s, hemophiliacs were at high risk of HIV infection. Now, new ways of making the clotting factors, along with improved testing of blood supplies, have almost eliminated that risk.

You may hear that you can pick up HIV from a toilet seat, from playing with other kids, or from sharing eating utensils with a person infected with HIV. Some people might tell you that you can get HIV from shaking hands with a person infected with the virus, by drinking from the same water fountain, or by using the same computer.

HIV *cannot* be spread in any of those ways. The virus can't get through skin without an opening, such as a cut or a sore. HIV quickly dies outside the body. Lots of things can damage HIV or kill it outright, including chlorine in a pool, common household cleansers, heat, lack of moisture, and sunlight.

You can't pick up the virus from normal kissing, either. There is an extremely slight chance that HIV may be spread by deep kissing, but *only* if both people have open sores in their mouths.

Wrap-Up

HIV can be spread from . . .
- One person to another through injecting drugs with the same needle or syringe
- One person to another through sex
- A mother to her child before birth, during birth, or through breast-feeding.

HIV cannot be spread by . . .
- Insects that bite, such as mosquitoes
- Sneezing
- Kissing
- Shaking hands
- Playing with the same toys or games
- Donating blood
- Getting an injection in a hospital, doctor's office, or other health-care facility
- Coming into everyday (nonsexual) contact with an HIV-infected person.

This risk-taking rock climber clambers up a cliff high above the California coast. Knowing about risks is essential for making good decisions.

Chapter Two

Risky Behavior

Almost everything we do in life can be a little dangerous, but some things are more dangerous than others. Mountain climbing is more risky than walking on the sidewalk. Of course, that doesn't mean you can't break your leg walking to the store or that you'll definitely get hurt if you go mountain climbing. Understanding the risks involved in an activity allows you to make good decisions about what you will—or won't—do.

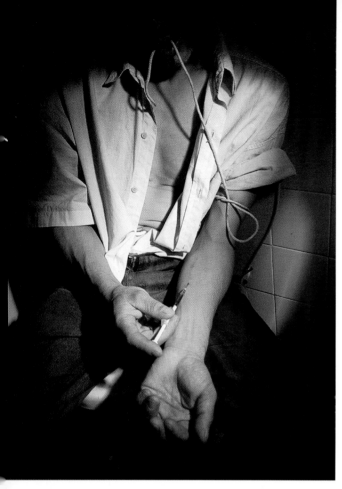

A drug user injects heroin into a vein in his arm. HIV passes readily from person to person when needles are shared.

Protecting yourself against infection from HIV is no different. Some activities pose only a small risk—but the risk is still there. Some activities are considered high risk. Every time you're involved in one of these high-risk behaviors, you may pick up HIV.

Intravenous Drug Use

You couldn't invent a faster way to pick up HIV than to inject yourself with a drug using someone else's needle and syringe. HIV infection is extremely common among **intravenous**, or IV, drug users—people who inject drugs into their veins.

Drugs commonly injected by IV drug users include anabolic steroids (drugs used to improve athletic performance); cocaine (also known as crystal, coke, and, when mixed with heroin, speedball); heroin (also known as black tar, H, horse, scat, smack, and snow); and phencyclidine (also known as PCP, angel dust, bust bee, cheap cocaine, and whack).

Here's how easily HIV can pass from one person to another through IV drug use. First, an HIV-infected drug user sticks a needle into his or her vein. Some of that person's blood cells—possibly carrying HIV—remain on the needle when it's taken out of the vein. Then someone not infected with HIV uses the same needle to inject drugs. At that moment, HIV particles from the first person pass from the needle into the second person's bloodstream, causing HIV infection. It's that easy.

To reduce the spread of HIV, many health centers have needle-exchange programs. Drug users can trade their used needles for clean, unused needles. Studies show that needle-exchange programs can cut the spread of HIV by up to 33 percent.

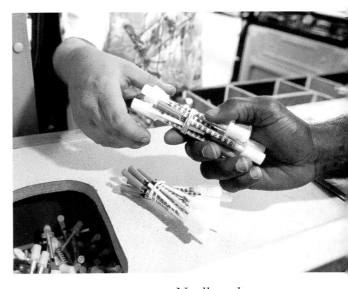

Needle exchange programs like this one let drug users trade dirty needles and syringes for clean ones.

Needle-exchange programs also reduce the spread of **hepatitis C** virus, another virus spread through blood-to-blood contact. A person infected with hepatitis C can suffer severe and lasting liver damage.

HIV in Seconds

Don't think contracting HIV can happen only when sharing a needle. You can also pick up HIV from sharing other sharp instruments to pierce an ear, a tongue, or another part of the body; to tattoo the skin; or to break the skin to share droplets of blood, as in a "blood brother" kind of ritual. Remember, all it takes is *one* blood cell carrying *one* virus particle to cause HIV infection.

Unfortunately, three teens from Pennsylvania found this out the hard way. Let's call the teens Jenny, Wanda, and

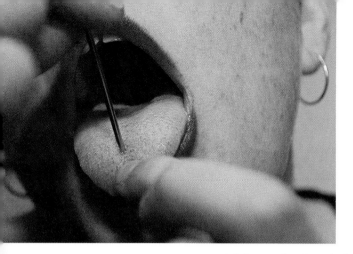

A woman demonstrates how a tongue piercing is done. Body piercing and tattooing can spread HIV unless the instruments used are completely free of germs.

Rachel. The girls wanted to pierce their tongues, so they went into a toolshed at Jenny's house. They found a sharp carpenter's tool they could use to poke holes in their flesh. Then they quickly pierced each other's tongue—first Jenny, then Wanda, then Rachel.

Although she didn't know it at the time, Jenny was infected with HIV. She had sex once with her boyfriend and had picked up the virus from him. Rachel was lucky enough to escape being infected during the piercing, but 19-year-old Wanda was not as lucky. She is now infected with HIV.

Getting AIDS During Sex

Having sex with someone infected with HIV is another extremely high-risk activity. Although nearly all body fluids in an HIV-infected person can contain the virus, only blood, **semen**, **vaginal fluid**, and breast milk contain enough HIV to spread from one person to another. During sex, any exchange of semen or vaginal fluid can lead to HIV infection in the uninfected person.

If an HIV-infected male has sex with an uninfected female, the virus can pass from the male to the female. The virus can also pass from an infected female to an uninfected male during sex, though this happens less often. In recent years, however, HIV infection from heterosexual (male-female) sex has been occurring more and more often.

Boy Meets Girl

By 1992, about 12,000 people had developed AIDS as a result of male-female sex. By 1996, that number had multiplied by nearly four times.

Sex between males—one type of homosexual sex—is also an extremely high-risk behavior. In the early 1980s, doctors noted that a large number of gay men were infected with HIV. They quickly realized that the virus could pass easily from one male to another during sex. **Anal sex**, which involves sexual stimulation of the rectum, has proven to be particularly dangerous.

AIDS activists march in a demonstration in New York City to educate people about the dangers of HIV.

The doctors and their patients alerted people in the gay community about the dangers of HIV. Many concerned people got together to fight AIDS and formed education groups to teach gay men how to avoid HIV. As a result, the number of gay men who develop AIDS has been dropping dramatically for several years.

High-Risk Rundown

- Main high risk behaviors for HIV include IV drug use and sex.
- A single HIV particle can cause infection.
- During sex, any exchange of body fluids can lead to HIV infection.
- HIV infection from male-female sex has been occurring more frequently over the last few years.
- Any activity in which body fluids might be shared can lead to HIV infection. One example of this is body piercing.

Decisions about sex can be difficult. We all want to trust the people we love.

Chapter Three

Cut Your Risk

Most teens say they understand the risks of using drugs or having sex, but understanding isn't enough. Decisions can be difficult. There's a lot of pressure to do the wrong things. Young people pressured to have sex or take drugs may begin to think:

- "Well, maybe it would be OK."
- "I know some guys are HIV-infected, but my boyfriend isn't one of them. I mean, he just can't be."
- "I hardly ever shoot up. Plus, I'm careful with needles, so I know I won't get infected."

- "Look, it's only this one time. What harm can there be in doing it just once?"

To avoid the risks of HIV infection, you need to realize that it could happen to you. Then take the next step: Do whatever it takes to avoid HIV completely.

That means *always* making wise decisions. One way—probably the best way—to help make sure you *can* make wise decisions is to stay away from alcohol. Alcohol affects the brain in a number of ways. It dulls the senses, particularly the

Alcohol can interfere with a person's ability to make proper judgments, increasing a person's risk of engaging in high-risk behaviors.

sense of touch. It throws off the sense of balance and slows the reflexes. Worst of all, it robs you of your good judgment.

Each time you drink, you increase your chances of making a decision you'll regret. That decision may involve a high-risk activity, such as using IV drugs or having sex. That decision may also be the one that eventually robs you of your life.

Drunken Decisions: Jose's Story

Eight out of ten teens first have sex under the influence of alcohol. Jose blames alcohol and its effects on his decision-making for his HIV infection. This is his story, in his own words.

"I thought I'd never catch HIV. I had a friend at work who was very skinny, and I kept teasing, 'You've got AIDS, AIDS, AIDS.' And now look at me. I'm the one who's got it.

"I blame drinking. I drank a lot and went out at night for some mischief, you know what I mean? To be with women. And I got HIV on the street. I was almost 19.

Life with AIDS is not easy for Jose, but he is relieved that his wife and children are not infected with HIV.

"[One day,] I was home taking a shower, and I couldn't breathe. They took me to the hospital. A doctor came into my room, and he told me, 'Jose, you have AIDS.' He said it like that, real blunt.

"I was quiet. I didn't say a thing. I was shocked, you know? I talked to [my girlfriend] Doris. I was very honest with her. I asked for her forgiveness. I didn't want to lose my family, my children.

"Thank God, neither she nor the kids have it."

Cutting the Risks of Sex

Jose didn't get infected with HIV from drinking alcohol. He was infected while having sex, a high-risk activity. To make sure you stay completely free of HIV through sex, you've got two options. Option one is to never have sex. Not even with the boyfriend who swears he doesn't have HIV or with the girlfriend you're "almost sure" has never had sex before. Never have sex with anyone, anytime.

Option two is to make sure—*absolutely* sure—that your partner isn't infected with HIV before you have sex. You can't be absolutely sure unless you and your partner have both been tested for the virus twice.

If the first test is **negative**, wait 6 months and then get tested again. In the meantime, you must not engage in any high-risk behavior with anyone. If the first and second tests are negative, for both you and your partner, then—and only then—do you have zero risk of getting the virus from sex.

If you choose to have sex and you're not absolutely certain that neither you nor your partner are infected, then at least keep your risk as low as possible by using a **condom.** Condoms help prevent the spread of HIV. If condoms are worn every time and used properly, the risk of exchanging semen or vaginal fluid is extremely low.

Most important, don't let anyone else pressure you into doing something risky. The decisions are yours to make. Remember, it's *your* health at risk.

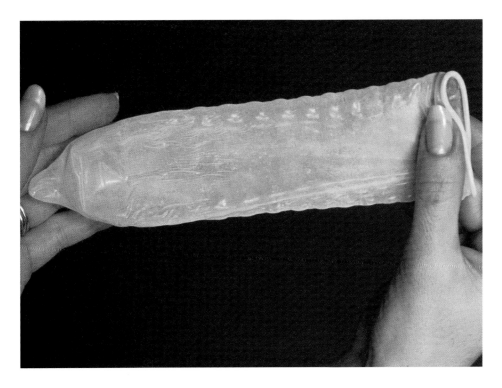

Properly used, a condom—like the unrolled condom shown here—can help protect against HIV.

Peer Pressure: Kerry's Story

Kerry became infected with HIV at age 15. While alcohol played a role in her infection, peer pressure—the desire to fit in—was the most important cause. This is Kerry's story, told in her own words.

"I was always seen as the most popular girl in my school. I would stand outside and people would just gather around me like I was some type of guru. It was a real hard role to live up to.

Kerry (purple shirt) exercises in front of a mirror. Kerry was infected with HIV when she was fifteen years old.

"Wanting to be liked by everybody led to drug and alcohol use, sexual involvement, and not knowing how to say no to somebody. I didn't want them to not like me.

"I ended up having sex with this guy. I didn't feel good enough about myself to tell him that I didn't want to have sex with him. I found out from another girl that he had HIV.

"I didn't believe her at first. I went to the doctor's office. He finally spoke up. 'You have tested positive for HIV.' It was like my whole world stopped.

"I just sat there, just absolutely horrified that this was happening. I thought that no one would ever want to hang around with me. I was never going to get married, and I was never going to have children. I was not going to grow old, and I wasn't going to have any normalcy in my life ever again."

Kerry died from an AIDS-related illness 3 weeks after her 22nd birthday.

A doctor writes on a patient's chart. Many patients with AIDS need intensive medical care for the cancers and infections they develop.

Chapter Four

Looking Ahead

AIDS can't be cured. However, many treatments available today are helping HIV-infected people to live longer. Doctors can now treat patients with a dozen or more anti-HIV drugs. These drugs are almost always given in combination. For instance, a patient with HIV may take three different drugs, each of which attacks the virus in a different way.

Some anti-HIV drugs stop the virus from making copies of itself. Others stop a cell from releasing copies of invading viruses into the bloodstream. Both kinds of drugs make it harder for HIV to overwhelm the body's cells, and it takes longer for signs of disease to appear. By combining drugs that use different methods of blocking HIV's operation, many people infected with HIV are in better health than they would be if they took drugs that attack the virus in just one way.

Doctors use a **viral load** test to determine how well anti-HIV drugs are working. The test measures how much HIV is in the blood. If a particular combination of drugs lowers a person's viral load, that person is less likely to develop AIDS within the coming year. The newer anti-HIV drugs have lowered the viral load of thousands of HIV-infected people. Those people have lived longer than they might have if the drugs weren't available.

The Downside of Treatment

Because anti-HIV drugs are almost always given in combination, a person may need to take dozens of pills each day. The pills must also be taken exactly on time. A delay of even 1 hour may be enough to give the virus a chance to gain a foothold in the body.

Anti-HIV drugs can cause severe side effects, too. In addition to a decreased number of white blood cells, which makes it hard for the body to fight infection, a person taking anti-HIV drugs might have too few oxygen-carrying red blood cells (a condition called **anemia**). The drugs can cause kidney stones as well as other forms of damage to the kidney, liver, or

Costly Care

A teen with HIV may need to take more than a dozen drugs two, three, even four or more times a day. Anti-HIV drugs and other essential drugs can cost as much as $60,000 a year— about the cost of two brand-new minivans.

These HIV-infected men display the drugs they take each day to fight HIV. Anti-HIV drugs can cost more than $1,000 a week.

pancreas. Some drugs can change the way the body distributes fat, giving affected people skinny arms, skinny legs, and a bulging stomach. Shifting fat around the body can also lead to high blood **cholesterol**, which increases the risk of heart attack or stroke. Other side effects of anti-HIV drugs include blurred vision, extreme weakness, headache, inability to sleep, nausea, vomiting, diarrhea, nerve damage, and rashes. A person with HIV may need to take other drugs to deal with all the side effects from anti-HIV drugs.

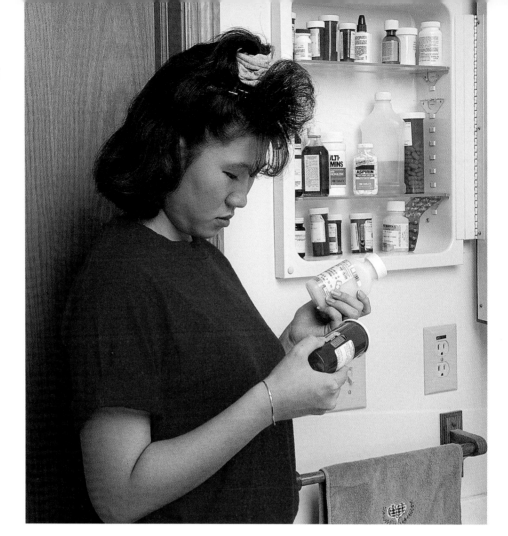

A teenager checks a pill bottle for information about side effects. Anti-HIV drugs can cause severe side effects, including anemia, kidney stones, blurred vision, nausea, vomiting, and weakness.

The Future of HIV Treatment

The recent success of the newer anti-HIV drugs may be only temporary. HIV can **mutate**, or change form, easily. Mutated forms of a virus sometimes behave differently than the original form. Doctors worry that as HIV mutates, the virus may become **resistant** to drugs that are currently effective. If that happens, the drugs won't work anymore and HIV will again begin to win the battle for the immune system in people with HIV infection.

Some doctors believe that they are seeing signs of this type of drug resistance already. They fear that the death rate from HIV infection may begin climbing again until the next wave of anti-HIV drugs comes along. Clearly, the only cure in sight is a cure readily available now—prevention.

Asking questions can help you gain important information about HIV and AIDS.

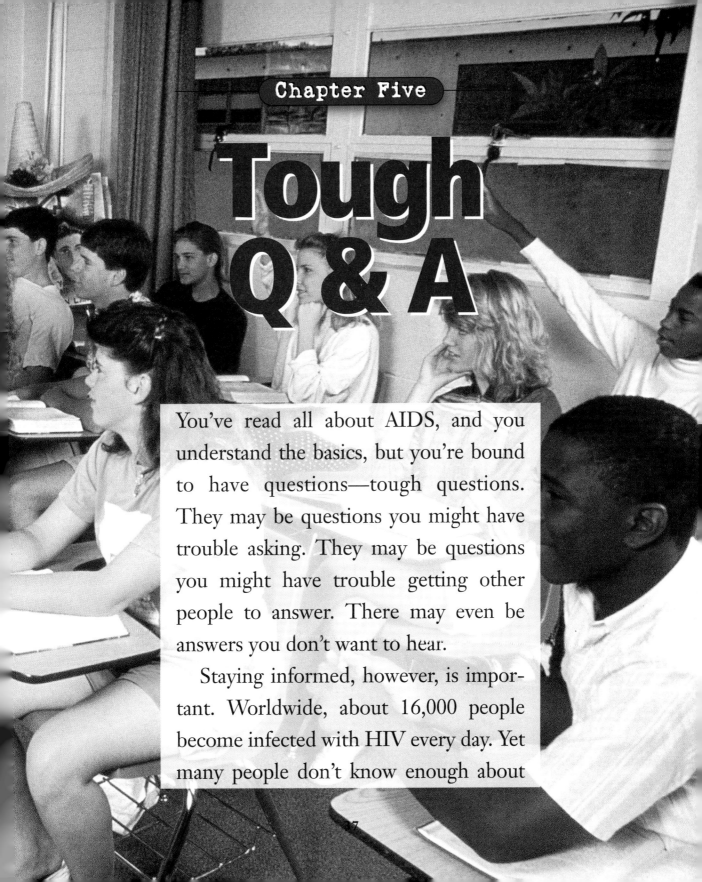

Chapter Five

Tough Q & A

You've read all about AIDS, and you understand the basics, but you're bound to have questions—tough questions. They may be questions you might have trouble asking. They may be questions you might have trouble getting other people to answer. There may even be answers you don't want to hear.

Staying informed, however, is important. Worldwide, about 16,000 people become infected with HIV every day. Yet many people don't know enough about

HIV and AIDS to understand the risks—or how to protect themselves. You should. You owe it to yourself, your family, and your friends to become informed.

This chapter asks some tough questions and then answers each one clearly and honestly. No games. No runaround. Just the facts. Maybe some of these questions are your questions too.

General Questions

Q: *What's the difference between HIV and AIDS?*

A: HIV, which stands for human immunodeficiency virus, refers to the virus that causes AIDS. AIDS, which stands for Acquired Immune Deficiency Syndrome, is the last stage of HIV infection. Everyone who has AIDS is infected with HIV, but not all people infected with HIV have AIDS. In fact, most HIV-infected people don't have AIDS. Chances are, however, that they will develop AIDS at some point.

Q: *When a person gets AIDS, does he or she die right away?*

A: No. HIV-infected people often live 10 years or more before the infection causes signs of AIDS. Most individuals survive at least 2 years after they first develop signs of the disease. In some cases, they survive even longer.

Q: *Where did HIV come from?*

A: Recent studies indicate that the main form of HIV in humans, known as HIV-1, most likely came from a certain kind of chimpanzee that lives in the African countries of Cameroon, Gabon, and Guinea. Researchers at the University of Alabama at Birmingham believe that humans contracted the virus while killing, skinning, and preparing to eat infected chimpanzees. A less common form of HIV, called HIV-2, most likely came from another species of chimpanzee.

Scientists think chimpanzees similar to the ones shown here were the original source of HIV.

Q: *Can you get HIV from a mosquito bite?*

A: No. Mosquitoes don't inject blood when they bite. They inject saliva. HIV can't survive in saliva.

Q: *I'm thinking of getting my body pierced or tattooed. Should I be worried about HIV?*

A: Professional tattoo and piercing parlors are supposed to **sterilize** the needles they use. That process kills germs, so that diseases cannot be spread from one person to another through the needle. Just because tattoo and piercing parlors are supposed to sterilize the needles doesn't mean they actually do or that they do it properly. If a friend offers to pierce your body, you have no way of knowing if the needle is clean. So say no. Make sure that any needle someone plans to use on your body has been properly sterilized.

Q: *Everyone I know says AIDS is a gay disease and affects only homosexuals. Are they right?*

A: No. AIDS is not a gay disease. During the mid- and late-1980s, the virus spread rapidly through the gay community, but today, the rate of HIV infection is rising fastest among heterosexual teens and young adults. Anyone can get AIDS.

Q: *If you are infected with HIV, do you have to tell the officials at your school?*

A: No. Only you and your family can decide who should be told about an HIV infection. On one hand, if you tell the school nurse about your infection, he or she might be able to take better care of you if you become sick at school. Often, a nurse is someone you can turn to for a kind ear and thoughtful advice.

A school nurse discusses AIDS with a student. Your school nurse can be a valuable source of information and thoughtful advice about sensitive issues.

On the other hand, you might consider the issue so private that you don't want anyone to know unless they absolutely have to. Either way, it's a decision only you and your family should make.

Q: *Can you tell by looking if someone is infected with HIV?*
A: No. HIV leaves no telltale signs. Hundreds of thousands of people infected with HIV are walking around right now. Each one looks perfectly normal because 8 to 10 years may pass before outward signs of HIV appear. In addition, as many as one-third of the people infected with HIV don't know it. So if they can't tell, how could anyone else?

Thousands of people walking the streets right now are infected with HIV and don't know it. If they can't tell they're infected, how could anyone else?

Questions About Relationships

Q: *If I have sex only one time, can I still pick up the AIDS virus?*

A: Yes. If your partner is infected with HIV, having sex even one time may be enough to contract HIV. The safest way to avoid HIV is to completely avoid having sex. If you do have sex, use a condom every time.

Q: *Shouldn't you trust your partner? I mean, I trust my boyfriend. He wouldn't lie to me.*

A: This isn't about trust. A virus doesn't care if you and your partner are nice, truthful people. Your sex partner may not even know that he or she is infected. If your partner has had sexual contact with anyone besides you or has been exposed to the blood of an HIV-infected person, he or she is at risk, and so are you.

On the other hand, if your partner hasn't been exposed to anyone else's blood and you're the only person he or she has ever had sex with—including oral or anal sex—you probably are not at risk.

Q: *What if you don't have sex, but you just fondle and massage each other? Is that safe?*

A: It's safer than sex, but it's not entirely safe. If two people want to become more intimate with each other without having sex, fondling and massaging may work for them. However, if they both have open cuts or skin sores and the sores come into contact with each other, HIV could pass from one to the other. If you and your partner have no cuts, scratches, or sores, fondling and massaging won't put you at risk.

Just be careful, however, that the fondling and massaging doesn't lead to **intercourse**. The desire to become intimate can quickly move from fondling to intercourse. And that, as you know, is most definitely *not* safe.

HIV doesn't care how much two people love one another. The virus can infect anyone who engages in a high-risk behavior.

Q: *What about oral sex? Is that safe?*

A: No, it isn't. In **oral sex**, contact occurs between the mouth of one person and the sexual organs of another. HIV in semen or vaginal fluid can enter the bloodstream through tiny cuts or open sores in the lining of the mouth.

Q: *Can condoms prevent the spread of HIV?*

A: Yes. Latex condoms help prevent the spread of HIV. If condoms are worn every time and used properly, the risk of exchanging semen or vaginal fluid is extremely low.

Latex condoms, like the ones shown here, can help prevent the spread of HIV.

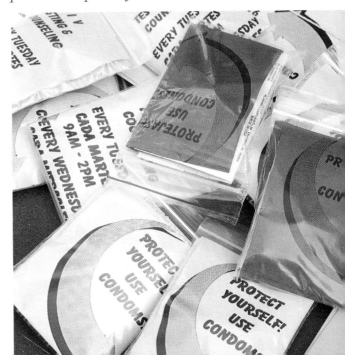

Keep in mind, however, that condoms are not fool-proof. They can leak. And if they are not used properly, they can allow semen to escape. In either case, HIV can spread from one person to another.

Q: *A friend of mine says that anyone who gets AIDS deserves it. I don't know what to say to her. I mean, in a way, they do deserve it, don't they?*

A: Kids like you all over the country are trying to make good decisions. But sometimes, no matter how hard they try, they make mistakes. We all do. Do they deserve to die because of one mistake?

Does a 17-year-old girl deserve to have her life destroyed because she once pierced her tongue for fun? Does an 18-year-old boy deserve to lose his life because he had sex with his boyfriend just once? What about a teen

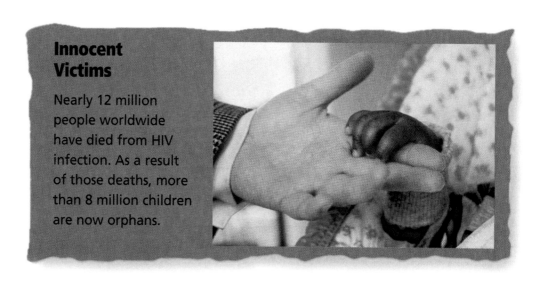

Innocent Victims

Nearly 12 million people worldwide have died from HIV infection. As a result of those deaths, more than 8 million children are now orphans.

who was sexually attacked by someone infected with HIV? Does she deserve the disease?

No, of course not. No one deserves to have AIDS.

Q: *Listen, if I wind up getting HIV from sex or something, I'm the only one who's affected. I mean, I'm the one who has to deal with it, right?*

A: Wrong. HIV places tremendous stress on your family. It affects your friends, neighbors, and classmates. It changes who you are, and who you are affects everyone you meet. That makes AIDS everyone's disease.

Questions About HIV Testing

Q: *I've never had sex and have never taken IV drugs. Do I still need to be tested for HIV?*

A: If you've never had sex, never taken IV drugs, never been so sick or injured that you needed a blood transfusion, then no, you don't need to be tested. You're not at risk for HIV.

Q: *I know someone who had sex with a stranger and then got tested for HIV a month later. The test was negative. Is she in the clear?*

A: Not yet. It can take 3 to 6 months for a person to test positive after being exposed to HIV. Your friend could test negative now, but in another month or two, she may test positive.

Questions About Treatment

Q: *With all the new anti-HIV drugs out there, AIDS is going away, right?*

A: No, AIDS is not going away. The new anti-HIV drugs are helping many people with HIV live longer, healthier lives, but HIV is a crafty virus. It can change form, or mutate, easily and quickly. Scientists are already seeing signs that the virus is becoming resistant to some anti-HIV drugs. If this trend continues, the death rate from HIV will most likely climb once more.

Q: *I've heard that the treatment for HIV is worse than the disease. Is that true?*

A: All anti-HIV drugs can cause side effects, and some of the side effects are severe. Many patients, however, can take the drugs for long periods without major problems. In any case, researchers continue to search for anti-HIV drugs that have fewer side effects.

Q: *If you're pregnant and infected with HIV, can you give the virus to your baby?*

A: Yes. HIV can pass from a pregnant mother to her child before or during childbirth, or when breast-feeding. A recent study, however, shows that delivering babies by an operation called a **cesarean section** can reduce the risk of HIV in the infant by as much as 87 percent.

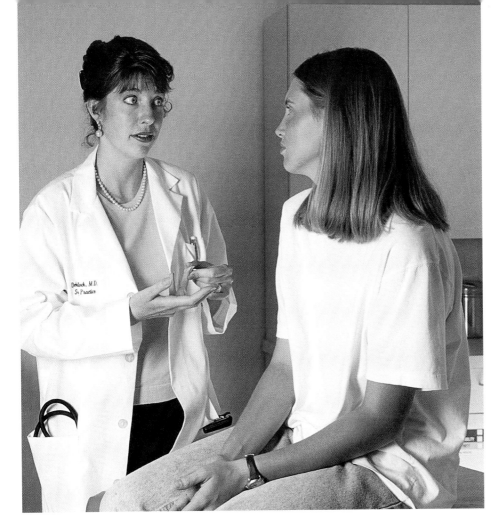

A doctor stresses a point when talking with a teenage patient. Doctors and other health care professionals play a large role in educating people about HIV and AIDS.

Q: *Will there ever be a cure for AIDS?*

A: Possibly. But scientists say they need to find a way to prevent the virus from infecting people and causing disease. Vaccines are now being studied that might help treat or prevent HIV infection. In the meantime, we need to do whatever we can to prevent the spread of HIV. Understanding AIDS and keeping yourself free of the AIDS virus is a step in the right direction.

It's a step we all need to take.

Timeline of AIDS

1981	The first AIDS case is reported to the Centers for Disease Control and Prevention (CDC).
1984	The human immunodeficiency virus (HIV) is identified as the cause of AIDS.
1985	The first test (ELISA) is approved for detecting the presence of HIV. AIDS-related death of movie star Rock Hudson raises public awareness. Blood banks begin to test all blood products for HIV.
1987	The first drug (zidovudine) is approved for use in patients with AIDS.
1988	Regulations are put into effect to help speed new HIV treatments to patients.
1991	Basketball superstar Earvin "Magic" Johnson announces that he is infected with HIV.
1996	The first protease inhibitor drug is introduced. The number of deaths from AIDS-related illness drops 44 percent in the following year.
1998	Scientists determine that the earliest known case of HIV infection occurred in an African man in 1959. A total of 54,407 AIDS cases are reported to the CDC between July 1997 and June 1998.
1999	Scientists determine that HIV might have come originally from chimpanzees.

Glossary

AIDS (Acquired Immune Deficiency Syndrome)—a disease of the body's infection-fighting system caused by human immunodeficiency virus (HIV)

anal sex—sexual stimulation between one person's sex organs and the rectum of another person

anemia—a condition in which the blood contains too few red blood cells; the most common side effect of anti-HIV drugs

cesarean section—an operation performed on pregnant women to remove the infant through the abdomen

cholesterol—a fatlike substance found in animal fats and oils. High levels of cholesterol can lead to blockage of an artery, which can cause heart attack or stroke.

condom—a latex sheath that fits over the penis during sex and prevents the exchange of body fluids

49

contagious—spread from one living thing to another

contract—to become infected with

direct contact—physical touching of the blood or other body fluids of one person with that of another

genital tract—the part of the body involved with reproduction; consists mainly of the vagina and uterus in a female and the penis in a male

hemophilia—a blood disease in which the blood doesn't clot properly

hepatitis C—a liver disease caused by hepatitis C virus. In hepatitis C, the liver can become so damaged that a liver transplant is the only option.

human immunodeficiency virus (HIV)—the virus that causes AIDS

immune—protecting against infection

incubation period—the period between the time a person is infected with HIV and the time when outward signs of HIV infection appear

intercourse—sexual contact that involves the genitals

intravenous—through the vein. People who use intravenous drugs are at increased risk for HIV.

Kaposi's sarcoma—a rare form of skin cancer that occurs primarily in people whose immune systems have been severely damaged

macrophage—a type of white blood cell that engulfs (swallows) viruses and bacteria and then destroys them

mucous membrane—the slimy tissue covering the inside of the mouth, nose, and other parts of the body open to the outside

mutate—to change form. HIV mutates quickly and easily, which makes treatment extremely difficult.

negative—showing that a disease is not present

nucleus—the part of a living cell that contains the cell's genetic information

oral sex—sexual stimulation between one person's mouth and the sex organs of another person

Pneumocystis carinii **pneumonia**—a rare lung infection that occurs primarily in people whose immune systems have been severely damaged

positive—showing that a disease is present

protein—a substance found in all plant and animal cells

resistant—able to withstand an attack

semen—the thick fluid in the male that carries sperm and is released during a sexual act

sterilize—to clean thoroughly to kill germs

T cell—a type of white blood cell that identifies invading organisms and signals macrophages to kill them

transfusion—the injection of blood from one person's body into another person's body

tuberculosis—contagious bacterial infection that usually affects the lungs

vaginal fluid—a body fluid released by tissues in the vagina of a female

viral load—a test that measures the amount of HIV in the blood and helps doctors predict a patient's risk of developing AIDS

To Find
Out More

Books

Bartlett, John G., Ann K. Finkbeiner, and The Johns Hopkins AIDS Clinic. *The Guide to Living with HIV Infection: Developed at the Johns Hopkins AIDS Clinic.* Baltimore: The Johns Hopkins University Press, 1998.

Morgan, Bill. *The Magic: Earvin Johnson.* New York: Scholastic, Inc., 1991.

Rathus, Spencer A. and Susan Boughn. *AIDS: What Every Student Needs to Know,* second edition. Fort Worth, TX: Harcourt Brace College Publishers, 1994.

Roleff, Tamara L. and Charles P. Cozic (editors). *AIDS: Opposing Viewpoints.* San Diego: Greenhaven Press, 1998.

Ward, Darrell E. *The AmFAR AIDS Handbook: The Complete Guide to Understanding HIV and AIDS.* New York: W. W. Norton & Co. 1999.

Watstein, Sarah Barbara and Karen Chandler. *The AIDS Dictionary.* New York: Facts on File, 1998.

White, Ryan. *Ryan White: My Own Story.* New York: Signet, 1992.

Zuger, Abigail. *Strong Shadows: Scenes from an Inner City AIDS Clinic,* New York: WH Freeman and Co., 1997.

Organizations and Online Sites

The AIDS Treatment News Internet Directory
http://www.aidsnews.org/aidsnews/index.html
This site provides links to AIDS treatment information, AIDS-related organizations, as well as programs and services for people with AIDS.

Campaign for Our Children
http://www.cfoc.org
This site provides information for teens, parents, and teachers about sex-related issues including pregnancy, HIV, and sexually transmitted diseases.

The Centers for Disease Control and Prevention Information Network
http://www.cdcnpin.org
This site offers a wealth of information and resources about HIV and AIDS.

The National AIDS Hotline
This hotline, run by the Centers for Disease Control and Prevention, is the primary HIV and AIDS information resource for the United States.

Planned Parenthood Federation of America, Inc.
This organization has information about HIV and how it spreads through sex. Ask for these pamphlets: *AIDS/HIV: Questions and Answers* (item number 1688), *Teen Sex? It's OK to Say: No Way!* (item number 1592), and *The Condom: What It Is, What It Is For, How to Use It* (item number 1550).

The Red Cross
http://www.redcross.org/hss/HIVAIDS
This site provides basic information about AIDS as well as a variety of books, posters, and products available from the Red Cross.

The Ryan White Foundation

http://www.ryanwhite.org

Ryan White was a ground-breaking Indiana teen with hemophilia who died of an AIDS-related illness when he was 18 years old. For the last 5 years of his life, Ryan battled for acceptance in his community and in so doing, inspired millions of people with his bravery.

Teen Sexuality in a Culture of Confusion

http://www.intac.com/~jdeck/habib

This unique site offers a collection of photographs and personal stories about teenagers and their struggles with growing up. The stories, in the teens' own words, originally appeared as a special series of articles in the *Concord Monitor* and *Portsmouth Herald*.

A Note on Sources

Dozens and dozens of books have been written about AIDS, tens of thousands of articles have been published, and hundreds of thousands of Internet sites have been built to deal with this important topic. It was difficult to know where to begin, so I started at my local library.

Among the many important resources I found there was a collection of articles in the July 1998 issue of *Scientific American*. I also found an informative article in the March 1999 issue of *Esquire*.

The Internet was also helpful for my research. The Centers for Disease Control and Prevention site (*http://www.cdc.gov/*) was a good source for statistics on HIV and AIDS. I accidentally discovered one of the most moving Internet sites I've ever seen: the *Teen Sexuality in a Culture of Confusion* report (*http://www.intac.com/~jdeck/habib/*). Some of the stories about the teens mentioned in the book you're reading came from that report, which originally appeared in the *Concord Monitor* and *Portsmouth Herald.*

As I worked on this book, I spoke with a number of AIDS experts. An AIDS educator named Elaine Pasqua, who lost her mother to the disease several years ago, was my primary consultant. I was also fortunate to have met Lee North, one of the longest-surviving HIV-infected individuals in the world. Dr. James Oleske, a highly respected pediatric AIDS specialist from the University of Medicine and Dentistry of New Jersey, reviewed this book for accuracy. His feedback proved extremely valuable and I am thankful for his assistance.

Most of all, I wish to thank my loving wife, who put up with endless hours of my sitting at the computer, writing, and who, for some reason, loves me nonetheless.

—Andrew T. McPhee

Index

Numbers in *italics* indicate illustrations.

About the Author

Andrew T. McPhee is a managing editor at Springhouse Corporation, a publisher of reference books, journals, and software for nurses and doctors. Formerly an editor at Weekly Reader Corporation, Mr. McPhee earned a degree in nursing from the University of New Hampshire. He has won two Educational Press Association of America awards for writing and editing.

Mr. McPhee has written or edited more than 700 health and life science articles for kids. He has been writing about AIDS since the mid-1980s, has provided nursing care for HIV-infected patients, and won an acting award for his performance in a production of *Quilt: A Musical Celebration*, based on true stories from the AIDS Memorial Quilt.

Mr. McPhee lives with his wife, Gay, and their children in Doylestown, Pennsylvania.